W9-AZX-753

Spider Storch's
Teacher Torture

$$10 \times 9 = 90$$
$$10 \times 10 = 100$$

Gina Willner-Pardo
illustrated by Nick Sharratt

Albert Whitman & Company • Morton Grove, Illinois

Library of Congress Cataloging-in-Publication Data

Willner-Pardo, Gina.
Spider Storch's teacher torture/written by
Gina Willner-Pardo; illustrated by Nick Sharratt.
p. cm.

Summary: Joey Storch tries to be on his best behavior in order
to keep his third-grade teacher, Ms. Mirabella, from retiring.
ISBN 0-8075-7577-1 (hardcover)
ISBN 0-8075-7578-X (paperback)
[1. Teachers—Fiction. 2. Schools—Fiction. 3. Behavior—Fiction.]
I. Sharratt, Nick, ill. II. Title.
PZ7.W683675Spt 1997
[Fic]—dc21
97-6125
CIP
AC

Designed by Scott Piehl.

For Evan, who would love for someone
to show him how to make contact
explosives. —G. W.-P.

For Yvette. —N. S.

Don't forget to read...

Spider Storch's
Carpool Catastrophe

by Gina Willner-Pardo

illustrated by Nick Sharratt

Contents

1

Trouble

 My mom is always saying, "Joseph Wolfgang Storch, you are a wild animal!" My dad is always saying, "No, I will not show you how to make contact explosives!" My sister, Louise, is always saying, "Mom, make Joey stop!" My friend Zachary is always saying, "Think before you talk, Spider!" Ms. Mirabella is always saying, "Joey, sit down."

I mean, Ms. Mirabella *was* always

saying, "Joey, sit down." Until last week.

Last week Ms. Mirabella retired.

"She's been teaching third grade for twenty-three years," Mom said one night a couple of weeks ago. That day, the principal had announced that Ms. Mirabella would be retiring at the end of the month. "Can you imagine?"

"She's pooped!" Dad said.

Louise spooned mashed potatoes onto her plate. "She's leaving because of Joey," she said. "Ms. Mirabella hates Joey. She can't even wait till June."

"She does not!" I yelled, spitting mashed potatoes by accident.

"Gross!" Louise said.

"Will you clean that up please, Joey?" Mom said.

That's another thing Mom is always saying.

"You just wore Ms. Mirabella out," Dad said after I'd gotten the paper towels. "You made puttering around in the garden sound too good to pass up."

"She loved *me*," Louise said. "She let me take the attendance slips to the office and go to the supply room when we ran out of staples and glue. She always said, 'What a helpful girl you are!'" Louise watched while I tried to pinch up drips of mashed potato with wet paper towels. "I'll bet she can't

believe I'm even related to you,"
she said.

I concentrated on not smearing the
mashed potatoes around on the table.

"She does *not* hate me," I said. But
I wasn't as sure as I sounded. I
couldn't help remembering things.

Like the time Zachary
and Andrew and I tried
to light Mary Grace
Brennerman's hair on
fire. Zachary and
Andrew asked Mary
Grace questions about
gymnastics and who all the girls' best
friends were. They pretended to pay
attention when she answered. But I
was the one who held the magnifying
glass, so I was the one who got in
trouble.

Ms. Mirabella made me stay after school for a week. I had to write "I will never light anyone's hair on fire" fifteen times every day.

Or the time I hid under the sink in the boys' bathroom and Zachary and Andrew told Ms. Mirabella I'd been kidnapped by three men with guns. Unless my teacher left a hundred dollars in a paper bag under the bench at the bus stop, I'd be history. Ms. Mirabella might have even believed them if Zachary hadn't said that one of the men had a sword and was wearing an eyepatch.

Ms. Mirabella made me stay after school another week. I had to write

"I will never pretend to be kidnapped" twenty times every day. And I had to sit on the bench at lunch recess.

The time when Travis Hoffberg had to be rushed to the emergency room wasn't really my fault. I dared him to stick the raisin up his nose, but he thought of the marble all by himself.

Ms. Mirabella made me stay after school for two whole weeks. I had to write "I will never dare anyone to do anything dangerous" twenty-five times every day. In cursive.

No matter how much I have to write stuff down, though, I can't seem to stop doing stupid things. I try. But I just can't help it.

When Ms. Mirabella gets mad, the tip of her nose turns pink. Pieces of gray hair that won't stay in her barrette fly all around her head. One of the veins in her neck gets big. But she never yells. I guess that's why I never thought she was that mad.

Or that she really hated me.

2

Ms. Mirabella

I didn't want Ms. Mirabella to hate me because I really liked her, even when she took points off my homework when I forgot to put my name on it. Ms. Mirabella was a lot better than Ms. Elliot, who got hives, or Mrs. Meredith, who smelled like cigarette smoke and mostly called on girls.

Ms. Mirabella thought of fun stuff

to do. She made up a rap song to teach us our times tables. "Hit it, Kenny," she'd say, and Kenny Baldridge would play drums on his desk and we'd all sing along with Ms. Mirabella:

Eight times four equals thirty-two.
You hear what I'm sayin', 'cause I'm
telling you.
Eight times five equals forty, I say.
It will tomorrow and it does today.

Sometimes Ms. Mirabella would even dance while we sang, but only when she was sure the principal was in a meeting and wouldn't be walking in.

Ms. Mirabella liked to keep interesting pets in

her classroom. Not just a goldfish, like in Mr. Bernstein's first grade. She had a terrarium full of tomato frogs on her desk. And she kept a bearded lizard named Vince in a big wooden cage near the windows. He ate live crickets. I liked to watch Vince chew them. Sometimes you could see their guts squirting out.

I was glad that Vince didn't eat spiders, because spiders are my favorite animals. I kept asking Ms. Mirabella if she could get a tarantula, but she said a lizard and frogs were enough.

Once Ms. Mirabella told us to pretend that *we* were the ones in cages and that Vince had to take care of us. We had to write down the things Vince would have to remember to do, like

change our sheets
and take us out
for bike rides.

One day about
a month ago, Ms.
Mirabella said
she had a special
treat for us. She brought her daughter,
Miranda, to school. Miranda was a
grown-up lady. She was going to have
a baby of her own. Her stomach was
huge. It looked like she'd stuffed a
balloon under her shirt.

Ms. Mirabella took a stethoscope
out of her purse.

"Who'd like to hear the baby's
heartbeat?" she asked.

We took turns listening to
Miranda's stomach. Mostly it sounded
like my stomach when I'm hungry.

Once I thought I heard a heartbeat,
though.

"Who wants to feel the baby kick?"
Ms. Mirabella asked.

I snuck looks at Zachary and
Andrew. We all thought it was
disgusting to have to touch some lady's
stomach that we didn't even know. But
everybody was lining up.

The baby kicked me right in the
palm of my hand. Hard. "Ouch!" I
yelled. Then, when everybody started
laughing, I shook my hand as if I were

trying to make it stop stinging.

Miranda laughed. "Ooh," she said. "That was a big one."

Ms. Mirabella nodded her head and smiled. "That baby knows a thing or two," she said. "That baby knows who he's dealing with."

Now, thinking about what Ms. Mirabella had said that day, I wondered what she'd really meant. Maybe she meant that baby knew he was dealing with a really crummy kid.

3

Spider Behaves

"I think it's my fault," I said. I was feeling really bad. It was recess, but I didn't even want to play chase or spy on girls.

"How come it's your fault, Spider?" Andrew asked.

"He *is* always doing dumb things without thinking," Zachary said.

"Yeah," Andrew said. "Maybe

Ms. Mirabella is retiring just so she can get away from you."

"Maybe we should do something," Zachary said. "I sure like Ms. Mirabella," he added.

"What would make Ms. Mirabella not want to leave?" I asked.

"Maybe if you quit causing so much trouble," Andrew said.

"And sat down once in a while without being asked," Zachary said.

I thought about it. "It might be hard," I said. "I'm used to being this way. I don't think I'd be very good at behaving."

"You could at least try," Zachary said.

All the next day I tried. Ms. Mirabella only had to tell me to sit down twice. And I only got in trouble

once, when I did karate on
the skeleton in the Science
Corner.

The next day I was
even better. At recess
I turned my eyelids inside
out, but I put them back the
right way before the bell
rang.

"Thank you for paying such good
attention today, Joey," Ms. Mirabella
said as she handed me my homework
ditto at the end of the day.

"You're welcome," I said.
Actually I was exhausted.
Behaving for a whole day
was tough.

The next day Ms. Mirabella
clapped her hands. "Class!"
she said. "I have a special

announcement to make."

Yes! I thought. I snuck looks at Zachary and Andrew. Ms. Mirabella was going to announce that she had decided not to retire. I knew it.

"A week from today we will be having a party in Room Six," Ms. Mirabella said.

Regina Littlefield raised her hand. "What kind of party?" she asked.

"A retirement party," Ms. Mirabella said.

Everybody groaned and booed.

"Now, now," Ms. Mirabella said. "No party poopers allowed!" She clapped her hands again. "Who knows what nine times seven is?"

4

Spider Tries Everything

"I guess behaving didn't help," I said after school. "Ms. Mirabella is still retiring."

"Rats," Zachary said. "I heard my mom say Ms. Schmidt is going to take over our class when Ms. Mirabella leaves."

Ms. Schmidt is a substitute teacher. She has long, pointy fingernails. She does not ever think anything is funny. Ever.

Ms. Schmidt is awful. But I felt relieved inside. Maybe I didn't have anything to do with Ms. Mirabella's retirement.

"Maybe Ms. Mirabella isn't leaving because she hates me," I said.

"Maybe she's bored," Andrew said. "I got bored when my dad made me take piano lessons. I locked myself in the hall closet and screamed until he said I didn't have to take them anymore."

"Maybe she *is* bored," I said. "Everybody's always asking the same old questions."

"'Can I get a drink of water?'" Andrew said.

"'Can I go to the bathroom?'" Zachary said.

"'What's this word?'" I said. "Maybe if we ask different questions, Ms. Mirabella won't be so bored."

The next day Ms. Mirabella explained about how to make a paragraph.

No wonder she is bored, I thought. She has been explaining about making paragraphs for twenty-three years. It was boring even once.

"Any questions?" she asked.

I raised my hand. "How many people live in China?" I asked.

"That's a very interesting question, Joey," Ms. Mirabella said. "How about if we look it up during Free Reading?"

"Okay," I said. I felt better.

After we sang the ten times table ("Ten times seven is seventy./Thirty-five for you and thirty-five for me."),

I raised my hand again. "Does the elephant eat the peanut *and* the shell, or just the peanut?" I asked.

"Let's stick to math, Joey," Ms. Mirabella said. "We'll look up elephants another time."

I tried again later. "How come some clouds are smooth and some are wrinkly?" I asked.

"Joey, please!" Ms. Mirabella did not look interested. She looked annoyed. "Pay attention to our discussion of pioneer schools!"

"You asked too many questions, Spider," Zachary said at recess. "Now she hates you even more."

"I was just trying to be interesting," I said.

"Maybe Ms. Mirabella doesn't like for us to be interesting," Andrew said. "Maybe she likes being bored."

"My dad said she's pooped," I said. "That she's retiring so she can rest."

"Maybe if she could rest at school, she wouldn't want to leave," Andrew said.

The next day I put a note in the suggestion box first thing in the morning.

After snack recess Ms. Mirabella cleared her throat. "Someone has suggested," she said, "that Room Six institute nap time."

Everybody groaned.

"Now, class," Ms. Mirabella said. "Let's discuss this calmly. Someone evidently feels that the demands of third grade require a nap. How does everyone feel about this?"

"That it's stupid," Mary Grace Brennerman said.

"That whoever needs a nap is stupid," Travis Hoffberg said.

I raised my hand. "Maybe the person who suggested nap time didn't do it for himself," I said. "Maybe he did it for other people." I paused. "The old ones," I added.

"That's *really* stupid," Mary Grace said. "We're all eight or nine."

Ms. Mirabella smiled.

"Thank you to whoever made the suggestion," she said. "I think the class has reached consensus. We will try to muddle through without naps." She gave me a funny look. "Even the old ones," she said.

•

"Now you embarrassed her!" Zachary said.

"You called her old!" Andrew said.

"I was only trying to help," I said.

But I felt lousy. It seemed like I was just making everything worse. "I don't know what else to do," I said. "Behaving didn't help. Or being interesting. And I guess she doesn't want a nap." I sighed. "Or she's too embarrassed to say so."

"It's too bad *you* can't leave," Andrew said.

"Thanks a lot," I said. But I knew he was just feeling as bad as I was. And I was almost out of ideas.

5

No Wind

On Thursday I tried flattering Ms. Mirabella. I told her I really liked the way her shoes looked with her dress.

"Thank you, Joey," Ms. Mirabella said.

"And your legs look thinner," I said. "Have you been losing weight?"

The tip of Ms. Mirabella's nose got pink. "That's enough, Joey," she said. "Have you finished problem twelve?"

On Friday I brought my grandfather's pocket watch to school for Sharing. I read somewhere that you can hypnotize someone to do almost anything. Maybe I could hypnotize Ms. Mirabella to keep teaching.

"I am going to hypnotize someone, but I need a volunteer from the audience," I said. "How about you, Ms. Mirabella?"

The class clapped politely as Ms. Mirabella pulled a chair out from behind her desk and sat down. I stood in front of her and dangled my watch in front of her face.

"You are getting very sleepy," I said in a low, slow voice.

"Ve-e-e-r-r-r-y, ve-e-e-r-r-r-y sleepy."

Ms. Mirabella crossed her legs and smiled.

"Ve-e-e-r-r-r-y sleepy," I said.

Ms. Mirabella cleared her throat.

"Is anything happening?" I asked.

"I don't think so," she said.

"Could you try rolling your eyeballs back up into your head?" I asked. "That sometimes helps."

Ms. Mirabella uncrossed her legs.

"I don't think that I care to roll my eyeballs at the present time," she said.

On Sunday my family went on a picnic. Usually I love picnics. I can eat with my hands, and no one says anything. I can sit far enough away from Louise so I don't have to hear her chew. I get to have soda. I get to fly my kite.

But this ended up being a lousy picnic. Mom made sandwiches with

pita bread and smelly cheese instead
of fried chicken. There was fruit salad
instead of macaroni salad, and iced tea
instead of soda. I couldn't find any
spiders. There were a lot of bees
around. I tried to pretend that I wasn't
afraid of them, but Louise could tell
and laughed at me.

 There was no wind. None. Mom
held my kite, and I walked backwards
until the string was taut. Then I
turned and ran. I could hear my kite
skidding along the dirt behind me and
everyone yelling for me to stop
running because it was useless.

"Rats!" I said. I plunked down right where I was. My kite lay on the ground like an animal that had been hit by a car.

Mom walked up behind me. "Cheer up, Joey," she said. "This just isn't the right day for kite flying. We'll do it another day."

"But I wanted to do it today," I said. I felt like being unreasonable.

"I know," she said. "But you can't control the weather."

"Rats," I said, drawing in the dirt with my finger.

"Sometimes there's just no wind," Mom said, "and there's nothing you can do."

6

Please Don't Go!

On Monday I waited until school
was over. I didn't tell Zachary or
Andrew what I'd decided to do. I didn't
want them to try to talk me out of it.
Also, I was afraid they might *not* try
to talk me out of it.

It was weird being alone in Room

Six with Ms. Mirabella when I didn't have to be writing things on the board.

She was sitting at her desk, bent over her work. Some hair that had come out of her barrette was hanging down across her forehead. She was chewing on her lower lip with her front teeth. She looked like she was concentrating.

"Ahem," I said softly, so I wouldn't scare her, and she looked up and smiled.

"Yes, Joey?" she said. "Did you forget something?"

I cleared my throat. "Um, I came to see if I could change teachers," I whispered.

Room Six was very quiet except for Vince skittering off his log.

"Is that so?" Ms. Mirabella said. She folded her arms across her chest. "Which teacher would you like to have?"

"Ms. Elliot, I guess," I said. Hives were better than smelling like cigarette smoke.

"Well, Joey," Ms. Mirabella said. "I think Ms. Elliot's class is full. Besides, I thought you liked Room Six."

"It's okay," I said. "I just think I need a change, is all." What I wanted to say was, I love Room Six!

"If it's me," Ms. Mirabella said softly, "I'll be gone next week. That's not so long to wait."

She didn't look mad. But I couldn't tell if I'd hurt her feelings.

"Oh, it's not you," I said. What I wanted to say was, Please don't go!

"It's just . . ." I tried to stop myself, but I couldn't. "I thought that maybe if I went to another class, you would decide to stay!"

Ms. Mirabella pushed some hair out of her eyes, which looked very surprised. "Joey!" she said. "Why would you think that?"

"Because," I said, "you hate me." When she didn't say anything, I said, "Everybody knows you hate me."

Boy, did I feel rotten. It's hard to explain how rotten I felt. There's something about telling someone that you know she hates you that makes you feel like you're just about to burst into tears. Even if you never cry in front of anybody and are absolutely sure that you aren't going to now.

"Joey Storch!" Ms. Mirabella said. She stood up and came over to where I was. She put her hand on my shoulder, but I backed away. "What makes you think such a thing?"

"Because you're always telling me to sit down," I said. "And because I'm always doing crummy stuff and having to write on the board that I'll never do it again."

"That doesn't mean I hate you, for goodness' sake!" Ms. Mirabella said. "You're funny and smart and very imaginative, Joey. Why on earth would I hate you?"

"My sister says you hate the kids who don't behave," I said. I liked that Mrs. Mirabella thought I was smart. Wait'll I tell Louise, I thought.

"I like all kinds of kids. The funny ones especially. Sometimes the funny ones are a lot of work." Ms. Mirabella smiled. "I don't mind, though."

"Then how come you're retiring?" I asked.

"Remember my daughter, Miranda?" Ms. Mirabella asked. "She had her baby last week. A sweet little baby girl."

"Oh," I said. "That's nice."

"She was born a little early," Ms. Mirabella said. "Miranda needs some help at home." She smiled. "I was planning to retire at the end of the year anyway. I just decided to leave a little sooner."

"So it really wasn't me," I said.

"Of course not, Joey," Ms. Mirabella said.

Ms. Mirabella was leaving and it had nothing to do with hating me.

"Don't forget about my party," Ms. Mirabella said.

"I won't," I said. "I don't feel like going to a party, though."

"Parties are a good way to say goodbye," Ms. Mirabella said. "Even when you don't feel like going to them."

7

Saying Goodbye

It wasn't just kids at Ms. Mirabella's party. The whole auditorium
was full of people. Louise thought she
was going to be such a big shot
because she hadn't had Ms. Mirabella

for two years. But there were grownups in the auditorium who had had her when they were eight.

A crowd of them was standing around Ms. Mirabella. They were talking about what it was like to be in her class.

"Remember me, Ms. Mirabella?" one lady asked. She was holding a baby on her hip. "I'm Sarah Beth Whitney. Remember?"

"Well, how are you, Sarah Beth?" Ms. Mirabella said. "Of course I remember you." She crossed her arms over her front and pretended not to smile. "No handcuffs, I see!"

"I can't believe you remember!" Sarah Beth Whitney said.

"In all my years of teaching," Ms. Mirabella said, "you were the only student who handcuffed herself to her desk." She laughed. "Of course I remember."

"I bet you don't remember me," a man with a beard said.

Ms. Mirabella looked at him as though she were trying to picture his face without hair.

"Roy Rutherford!" she said. "The boy who ate five sticks of chalk! How are you?"

Roy Rutherford looked embarrassed and proud at the same time. "Better now," he said. "Boy, was I sick!"

Ms. Mirabella smiled. "I've never forgotten

you, Ms. Mirabella," Roy Rutherford said. "I have some very happy memories of being in your third grade."

"I'm so glad, Roy," Ms. Mirabella said.

Lots of grownups came over to talk to Ms. Mirabella. Most of them remembered doing something crummy. One man said he kept an applesauce jar full of spit in his desk until Ms. Mirabella found it and made him throw it out. A lady remembered telling Ms. Mirabella that the Russians had bombed Minnesota.

Some of the grownups went to the refreshment table. Ms. Mirabella saw me standing by myself and came over.

"What are you thinking, Joey?" she asked.

"That all those grownups did all those lousy things," I said. "I wonder if my parents ever did stuff like that?"

"I wouldn't be surprised," she said.

Then she did a funny thing. She looked over both her shoulders, as if she was making sure that there was no one behind her who could hear our conversation. Then she leaned down close.

"I'll tell you a secret," she whispered. "I was the kind of kid who couldn't behave."

"You!" I said.

I couldn't picture Ms. Mirabella as a kid who couldn't behave.

I couldn't picture Ms. Mirabella as a kid.

"That's hard to believe," I said.

"It's true," Ms. Mirabella said. She sounded proud.

I still wasn't sure she was telling the truth. "What was the worst thing you ever did?" I asked.

She thought for a minute. "I smuggled a firecracker into school and hid it under a pile of dog doo out on the playground," she said. "I blew that dog doo sky high," she added.

I laughed. It was weird hearing a teacher talk about dog doo.

"Mr. Swift was the principal. Some of the flying dog doo stuck to his glasses," Ms. Mirabella said.

"Wow," I breathed.

Ms. Mirabella was staring into the distance. "It was really something," she said.

"That was worse than anything I ever did," I said.

Ms. Mirabella looked at me. "It was, wasn't it?" she said.

After a minute she said, "So how could I hate a kid who never did anything as bad as I did?"

"Yeah," I said. "How could you?"

For a minute I felt better. Until

I remembered that Ms. Mirabella was leaving. If I weren't a kid who was absolutely sure that I would never cry in front of anyone, I would probably have burst out sobbing.

I'll miss you, I thought.

"Do you still like firecrackers?" I asked instead.

"Oh my, yes," Ms. Mirabella said. "And sparklers and Roman candles and bottle rockets. All that stuff."

"You don't know anything about contact explosives, do you?"

I knew she wouldn't tell me anything, even if she did know. But I had to ask.

"Nothing I'm planning to share with you at the present time," Ms. Mirabella said. She smiled a little smile. Her eyes were shiny.

I knew that was Ms. Mirabella's
way of saying that she would miss
me, too.